A Strangled Heart

Also by Isabella Juanita Lyn
Everything I Couldn't Say

A Strangled Heart

Isabella Juanita Lyn

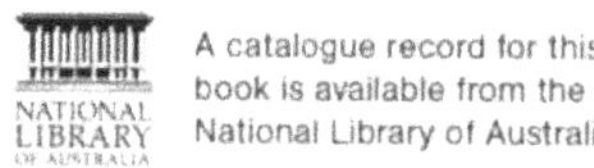

A catalogue record for this book is available from the National Library of Australia

For those who let their snake
taste their own venom

and to those who helped me
forget mine

The First Bite

After saying goodbye

Time felt slow,
despite it being six months later,
without the slightest care
to traumatise the only spark
haunting my mind.
The truth of a scarring memory
wasn't hidden;
an event all too great
for a single mind to recall.
You were the dimming light
in the cave of the islands.
The deeper I went in,
the greater the fear that tightened my bones.
Goodbye wasn't easy
but nothing in life was.
You were someone I thought

stayed

but you left faster than
the knots of wind messing
my hair on a speedboat.
Your plague disarmed me
feeling like humid weather
and I wasn't immune to the sweat.
Tears stung my face
almost incessantly as bees

gathered pollen and nectar in the spring.
I wished for a night,
clear from the memories of you.
But that night was still
a wish after saying goodbye —
now seven months ago.

You haunted dreams

The evening became my least favourite time of day.
I dreaded knowing that the darkness
held memories of you.
Goodbye was seven months ago,
enough time to forget and
enough time to erase
you.

But you haunted dreams.

The scars of that night — tonal ambiguity.

Diamonds were the strongest
but you stole my diamond heart
before the heist ceased.

I didn't want to think of you

Why did you enter my mind
when I needed you out of it?

I was out with my friends,
you were the lyrics I struggled to forget.

I was leaving work,
you became unforgettable melodies.

I was on another date,
you were him.

A ghost of my past life,
pale against the crimson rose in his hand.
His eyes were yours,
his smile —

identical.

I didn't want to think of you,
not anymore,
not any longer.

But my mind remembered

It remembered all those details
I tried to blur and erase.
The shade of your hair,
the light in your eyes,
the curve of your lips.

My mind remembered it all.

I wish I could forget,
I wish I could forget when you
slithered out of my life
but left your fangs in my heart.

Betrayed trust

What more was there to say?
You told me everything you needed
to coil the truth for your melody.

I was the song you couldn't find.
I was the song of twisted lies,
the one you sang to the top of the charts.

Trust eliminated,
my space abused
in the bars of
a small tune.

I was the chorus but the sincere bridge
starring you as the opening act.

You had to leave

Out of my life, mind, heart and soul.
I didn't need your presence
to torture me forever
in my sleep, work, songs and runs.

I didn't know how much longer
I could resist your grasp,
pretending you weren't tightening my heart.
But time wasn't placed on supposed ends.

Hide away

Like you promised when
we first met and said,

"If I broke your heart,

I'd let you go."

"If I hurt you,

I'd apologise until things were right."

"If I didn't tell you to change,

I'd be lying to you."

"If I kept you out of the spotlight,

It was for your own good."

My nightmare

Seven months after you
and I still couldn't sleep.
What spiteful world was this
where you couldn't earn your keep?

You covered me in restricting dust,
discomfort swirling through my green veins
then suffocating my only trust
and certainly, then did I combust.

Emulating the darkness from my dreams
seventeen		months			ago.
I didn't know those first
ten months was psychosis.

Coiled anguish

Burnt hearts.
I wish I had better memories
of our time together
but they were only fragments
of the bitter truth.

The caution tape caught swaying in the wind
behind you when you leaned in for a kiss.

Flashes of a warning siren
swallowed me whole
before I heard the

final

track.

Angered grief

Your cold blood is forever imprinted on my skin,
the fangs you left had me hooked.
I thought I escaped you when I broke it off
but you stoned my heart
like a Russell Viper's bite.

Restricted

You squeezed my neck,
tighter and tighter,
limiting my chance to escape.

Your fangs slashed into my trapezius,
deeper and deeper,
clutching me while devouring hope.

A disguised musician

You wrote a song about me,
a song your parents chastised you for.
This was your dream,
the career only I encouraged.

The late nights spent
writing, recording, producing
songs that one day would
take the world by storm.

Those afternoons after work,
laughing in the coffee shops
when an idea struck like gold and
you'd compose a melody from the sounds around.

You were always talented,
something your parents refused to believe.

The crystal snake in my nightmares was wrong.

I never wanted your creative spark to dull.

So blindly,
     your dreams,
          I followed.

Sponsoring and supporting every gig,
mastering your songs and running the surveys.

You were a born musical snake.

You got the record deal of your dreams,
you had the fanbase of an Inland Taipan,
you were the python of the charts.

But you stayed camouflaged to break my heart.

I couldn't breathe

I didn't think I'd see you again.

Caged inside your dream,
living through the corporate world
you failed to convince.

I couldn't breathe
when you trilled my name.
Time stopped, an illusion like modern poets
had us believe when it continued to pass us by.
I turned the other way,
my earphones in.

I couldn't hold you without the fear
of losing the only thing I craved.
More than life, you meant to me.

No one else was you, aria.

Hollowed inside out,
your song played on repeat inside my soul.
Your cologne was still strong,
minty and clean,
but not enough to wash her out of my mind.
You grabbed my hand,
my heel pivoted,

the boom-boom-boom thundering,
your eyes poised while you stared into my soul,
your lips danced a mischievous smirk.

"Still listening to my hit song, aria?"

CRACK!

The first bite

Lost for words, I stared at you.
Modulation...
You looked the same
except for the new haircut and stronger grip.

You took my earphones out,
grabbed my phone from my bag
and turned off the song.

"It's still my favourite too.
The song that propelled my career
and one I never regretted releasing."

"It was the song the crowd wanted."

I wish I didn't speak,
my voice cracked the cadence like a coda.

Your smile cured the wound in my heart
and small shards of glass vacuumed off the floor.
Encapsulated by you, your warm breath against my cheek
whispered into my patient ear,

"It was my love song to you."

Words caught in my throat,
your arm wrapping around my waist
as my knees gave way.

"I missed you,
losing you was my biggest mistake."
You whispered to my lips,
"Can I kiss you?"

If this was my fairytale,
I never wanted to hit pause on this aphrodisiac rhapsody.

The Second Bite

Issues unresolved

Your cologne reminded me this was true,
this was reality, not another heartbroken dream.
You were here, me in your arms.

I still loved you despite the uproar
my mind fought daily.

I didn't want to lose you that day,
but how could I fathom the reason
you continued to be a star?

Your fame was a price I paid.

Your blissful lies

You were the only one who believed in me.

An empty guitar case, while others had notes and coins.
You were a struggling musician when we met,
playing covers on the sidewalk, hit songs,
but no one stayed to listen or even glanced your way.

Who could blame them?
A dog playing the piano wasn't the norm in small towns.

Sometimes I heard your stomach growling,
pity creasing sweat beads from my run.
I ran past you before,
but that day, the acoustics slithered into my ear.

The tune spun my heart,
heavy breaths receding.
I didn't want to stop listening.

Afterwards, we had a coffee
and you told me about your dreams.
"How about you, aria? What dreams ran wild
in such a beautiful mind?"

How could I have said I didn't have one?

A small smile drew my lips, cheeks red.
"I still don't know. I recently moved to the town

from the country to study.
I haven't chosen my degree yet."

You smiled, sweet and innocent as the young day.

"The fame's worthwhile,
the fans screaming your songs,
the touring,
the creativity, unbound."

And I considered for a moment.
                                    But not the creative aspects.

Was I wrong to pursue a career as a manager?
What about health science?

You placed a tip on the table, winking,
"Aria, call me modulation, my favourite word."
A napkin slid towards me.

He changed me.

It wasn't my original plan
but plans changed and I was willing
to change with you.

Your first single blew up.

I couldn't have done this without you.

Our date nights became studio sessions.
Recording promotions and new songs weekly,
hoping to ride out the tidal wave of your success.
It became our shared dream,
a dream I wanted to live in forever

with you.

I noticed the songs started taking a new direction.
They weren't only love songs anymore,
but ones that also channelled heartbreak.

Did you miss her?

Joy seeped in

I didn't remember that night
when your lips touched mine.

It felt like forever then.

I was on cloud nine,
somewhere I thought I had said goodbye to.

Your hands on my waist
returned me to reality.

I pushed you away.
Like a plague,
you lingered.

"I love you; I always loved you."

If only my heart didn't flutter...

Voice on replay

Your voice was on replay,
replacing the bittersweet melody
of the song you released
when we broke up.

I didn't think I'd be giddy
or hopeful that something,
something could still blossom.

But I was too wishful
until I heard your voice replay
the chorus where the venom rests.

Notes of a Hidden Love

To the aria in my heart,

I was forever grateful
when I saw you running that day.
I have visited that path since
the day you played our final chord.

I wished I never made that mistake,
you deserved better than me.
But I was too selfish to see,
and now, I couldn't let you go.

I planned on making it up to you,
another song to express my true emotions
and the love that I didn't fight for.
But I never thought it would end
the way it did.

I wished that I could be yours
and I hoped one day you'd let me again.
But until then,
I'll wait for your forgiveness.

Always, your modulation ♡

Lived Rent-free

You used to live rent-free in my head,
forever singing and playing your guitar
while I went about my day.

Now you were in my apartment
and I had no restraint,
singing your latest song.

You lived rent-free in my head,
but your songs stopped paying my mortgage.

Our song

I heard your guitar strumming next to me.
My eyes felt sticky, my hair damp.
Blankets surrounded me on my bed,
you played chords quietly as I awoke.

"Morning my aria. How'd you sleep?"
You placed a delicate kiss on my hair.

Was she prettier than me?
Did you still love her?
Did she kiss you in ways I couldn't?
Was she the reason your heart fluttered?

"Good."

I hadn't slept without nightmares of you
for the past seven months and now,
you were back in my apartment and life.

You promised you'd make things right.
You promised you'd stay loyal.
You promised she was non-existent.

And you kept them.

Everything you said stayed true.

But did you think about her when I was gone?

Were you still seeing her?
Was she nothing to you like I was back then?
Did you still want her?

My melody, the only song
my heart sang without a tone.
Your pink lips hid the anger
when I didn't wish you 'goodnight'.
How could I have been so blind
but now I'd do anything
and everything
to make my melody right.

You continued strumming your guitar,
I brushed my hair for the day.
I heard you singing outside the bathroom door —
it was our song.

On repeat

I remembered playing that song on repeat,
dancing and singing my heart out
before suspicions suffocated me.

It was my favourite song of yours.

The hours you spent huddled over a notepad,
scribbling and erasing lyrics that fit
one minute and not the next.

You wrote this song privately
as I typed emails and did my best
to find your next concert venue.

Your frustrations when the chords weren't arranged
or when you couldn't find the perfect word.
I remembered it all.

You held no doubts back then
and your success proved you right.

This song was the one.

Just like our love.

Wishful whispers

It was midnight,
our favourite hour.

The grass underneath felt warm,
our hands intertwined.
You pointed to the shooting star.

"Remember when you said that'd be me?"
"Forever, my modulation."
Your forehead touched mine,
your lips were cold, unlike the summer night.

"I made it, all because of you, aria."
Smiles graced our faces,
your eyes reminded me of a blue supermoon
or Halley's Comet.

I kissed your lips,
the cold touch turning heated,
your hands running through my hair,
tangling and weaving your next tune.

You weren't the wrong person, right time.
You were the right person, wrong time.

Hopeless strength

I loved twirling in your arms again,
I loved singing with you again,
I loved being with you again.

The heartache was worth it,
the seven months of pain only made us stronger,
we were right for each other.

Another "Young, Dumb, In Love"

You started writing a new song,
you called it "Young, Dumb, In Love".
The title was different,
nothing like your discography.

I returned my focus to my laptop,
setting up your recording software
while my eyes danced towards your notebook.

I prepared your favourite tea.

"To keep the vocal cords alive," you always said.

Laughter followed and I joined you at the piano.
You started playing in the key of G.
It was always your go-to key.
You started strumming,

strumming to the beat you chose.
I followed your lead,
composing a melody that choked my heart.
Another sad song?

The title made sense in a few weeks.

Wandering hopes

You knew to tighten your coil when I exhaled.

I hope

I hope I was wrong about you.
I hope the truth was different.
I hope history wasn't repeating itself.

The poison began leaking

You started arriving home after three am.
I never got a straight answer from you.
You started keeping secrets from me.

Again...

One month into a second chance
and you dropped the prey.

I never had a proper conversation with you.
Your presence came with the waft of other perfumes,
nice from afar but unappetising to ones without scales.

I never thought you'd do it again.

"No girlfriend, just me."

A shaken heart

I knew it was too good to be true.
I trusted you changed,
changed for the better.

You didn't.

You were still the lying, cheating snake
that clung to my heart only eight months ago.

Embraced.
                Gripped.
                                Clenched.

You caught more girls in the summer than in winter.

Surprised I fell for you then.

Scarred lyrics

A snippet of "Young, Dumb, In Love"
blessed my ears, while my heart
wished, begged, prayed
it wasn't the truth your soul
hid in plain sight.

Poignant lyrics, your specialty.
Soulful ballads, your flair.
Breaking hearts, your expertise.

Those scarred lyrics from your chorus
told me what you never could.
You didn't want me as a lover.

You wanted me as a song.

Broken tunes

You cut the recording when I walked in.
I knew what song you were singing,
the chords stuck diligently in my mind,
the melody smothered me knowing it was mine.

The discordant tune I heard playing back,
your hand slamming against the keys
while the microphone fell apart.

"Sorry, it's not finished yet."

Out of my mind

I ran out of my apartment.

I needed space from you.

I couldn't pass by other women,
unable to see a blurred her.
You had been living a lie with me
while flirting with the town behind me.

I needed to get you out of my mind
and out of my life.

Thrill ÷ Loyalty

I loved you because of you,
you loved the songs I held for the chart-topping thrill.

I hated you because of secrets,
you hated me because of symphonic loyalty.

You sought for tunes, evoking thrill over loyalty,
shrouded behind the orchestral cacophony
while I hummed the dictionary and thesaurus
searching for the next harmony.

But I kept circling back to one.

Disgust wasn't a word
in my dictionary.

It was an image of you.

The second bite

I gave you a second chance
and you used it like the first.

You strived for your fame,
strangling anyone who got in the way,
and coiling those who appeared as obstacles.

I wasn't someone who got in the way
nor was I someone who became an obstacle to you.
I was the song,

the song you couldn't sing after I left.

When we broke up,
I called you a selfish pigeon.
Ironic, considering snakes ate pigeons.

The second bite hurt more than the first.
I was ready to say goodbye when suspicions arose.
But I had broken
faith in you.

You proved that you weren't worth my love
and I was ready to give someone my all.

I wish it was you.

The Third Bite

Was I psychotic?

I didn't slam the door on you.
I knew I should've, but I couldn't,
not again.

Was I psychotic
for convincing myself
that you could change,
love, and stay?

It wasn't healthy to hold on,
especially to poison,
but those memories and the potential
made it worthwhile until tonight.

Was I psychotic
for hoping you
weren't a jerk or another cheater
who would learn right from wrong?

Yes, I was psychotic.

Were you psychotic?

I knew there was more
than what you told me.
Did you love someone else?
Did you find me boring?

Were you psychotic for thinking
I'd change to fit your pretentious life
or to assimilate into your world
to stand on the stage but behind the curtains?

I didn't want to leave
the first night I caught
you with your tongue down her throat.
But I knew I wanted you gone
the second time I smelt her perfume.

Was there an us?

We never existed as a team,
a team who loved and
supported each other.

It was the musician

and the manager.

A famous guy

and an unknown girl.

It was you

and me.

We were an 'us' at the start,
but the start was point-five centimetres per second
times infinity behind.

Psychopath entered

There were no tears this time around.
You didn't need to waste my energy
and I couldn't stop the thought of
you and her kissing in the bar
from slithering in and out.

Your eyes haunted my sleep
and the curve of your lips on mine
was never forgotten.
The way your hands held my waist
as we danced under the moonlight
and your cologne I branded
was forever imprinted.

Now it was her instead of me.

On the radio

Your song played again
and I tuned into silence.
I hated driving,
hated it since we broke up
the first time,
loathed it the second time.
Your songs played so often
and I knew the company loved you.
I knew you would become the star
I helped brand and market.
But that star held secrets
that no one would know,
song or not.

Was I a game to you?

You played me like your piano.
Complicated but simple
with the waltz of death in the walls.

Was I a game to you?
Or another melody to remix...

You always refused to collaborate with other artists
and I wondered why when
you never questioned my decisions.

I haven't listened to your songs
since the night I kicked you out.
But your profile is hard to miss
and the billboards didn't help
me hide and run away.

I saw your latest song title,
the one we wrote together,
and now you released it
with another girl
singing my part.

You didn't care

Asking you to remove it
would've been like asking for a non-cheating guy.
You didn't care about my feelings,
expressing your sadness in the lyrics
you added from the aftermath.
I did and didn't love you
but this song made me wish
that you still called me your aria.

I shouldn't have cared either.
You were *modulation* after all.

Merciless

You played ruthless
games with only one victor —
you,
         you,
                  always you.

Did you love me or her?

I wanted you to love me
and forget that she existed.
But if that was true,
I'd be a lie
and another song under your name.

Mocked

You released another song the following week
and I wondered why I listened.
Why did I feel the pull so strong
to know about your every move in the industry?

I left, found a new corporate job,
and distanced myself from the music world.
I was never getting back into it again.
I didn't want to manage another musician.

Your lyrics were mocking,
the passive-aggression towards my new industry.
Why couldn't you let it go and
leave me alone?

Remember when you said you'd "hide away"?

I didn't forget trust

Singing that I was the one who writhed your heart
when you were the reason for our demise —
pathetic in my books.
I shut my laptop and tuned into the quiet of my room.

It was too quiet.

I hadn't played the guitar since I was young,
before you released your first single.
I missed the strings,
the plucking and strumming motions to create sound.
I played a C chord,
the foreign electric current running through my bones.
The other perspective to your song
became the lyrics in an instant.

Hide away you said,
I wish you kept the
promise you made.

You fed me lies again
and again, acting
like the hard truths were
non-existent to

us.

Love, such a cruel word;
hope, an innocent blossom;
destruction, the end to all.

Your eyes, mind, smile —
I couldn't read them
to know what you were thinking.

Your songs, lyrics, disguises —
I burnt them and breathed in the ashes
of the spark in the graveyard of an untold love.

Your effect on me had hardened my heart,
the piano played melodies
that sang a ballad for the loss of
Romeo and Juliet.

The only difference was our fate.

Did you find pleasure in my pain?

I saw you in my favourite store today.
You picked up the last bouquet
of the pink roses I bought weekly.
Your lips, smirking.

Venom danced in my veins

The piano became my best friend.
The studio still smelt like your cologne,
minty and clean.
I aired the room daily
but your scent still strangled me.
Venom danced in my veins
as lyrics flowed out of my brain.
Would it hurt to release these songs?
Success wasn't a one-way street
and connections were more than plenty.
The image of you kissing her twirling in again
and I sent that message to your producer.

Were you the end of me?

Or was I the end of you?

Pain deep in bones

I used to dwell after the first breakup
if you'd call and ask me to come home.
But I didn't want my old home anymore.

The pain soon turned to revenge
and revenge turned to love.

A love for songwriting.

I never liked playing instruments or writing,
let alone performing those words to anyone.
It seemed pointless
and I wasn't one to be creative with my time.

But now, my hours chorused words I never could.

A heartbroken quest

More like the quest of heartbreak
turned into a quest for asphyxiation.

You were trauma in a person

Every night, the image of you and her kept me up.
I didn't sleep as well as I did.
I hoped that would fade as the songs increased.
But I'm at song twenty and you were still there.
I haven't left my apartment in days.
The heavy eyebags concealer couldn't hide
and the weight on my shoulders
creating the female version of the Hunchback.

You were trauma.

Facts downplayed

You downplayed the facts in your song
when my album released.
Your counterargument, another that didn't reach your
toppers.
My songs were rising on the charts,
surpassing some of your songs.
Even my favourite.

I smiled when I saw you take the last bouquet again.

I grabbed the white roses,
paid,
dyed the petals pink,
and set them alight.

Aria stopped crying to your voicemail.

Fangs sank deep

Your fangs in my heart sank deeper.
I shouldn't have gone to the bar to celebrate
but why didn't the town build a second bar
for people to avoid each other?

Small-town problems...

Your hands were all over her,
buttons half-undone while she pressed you
further into the dark corner of the building.

My dinner almost came up at your feet
and I left before my hangover
was witnessed by you.

A new song was coming tonight.

Venomous melodies

The guitar sounded more poignant than usual.
I didn't stop the stream of consciousness
that overflowed my mind,
clouded by the shots I downed.
You told me you weren't a drinker
and I stopped consuming alcohol.

But alcohol made melodies venomous.

You poisoned hearts

Modulation,
I was another heart
that you couldn't love.

Modulation,
I was lovesick but you,
you found me monotonous.

Modulation,
you poisoned hearts
and they became my songs.

Sick to my stomach

I heard your latest single,
another non-chart-topper.
I could sense your frustration.
Oh well, my latest single was holding strong.
First place, why, thank you!

I didn't celebrate at the bar this time.
I wanted a wholesome dinner with my team
at my favourite restaurant.

But you were on a date with her
and I felt sick to my stomach.

Poisoned kisses

I never knew that a smirk
could've constricted my airways
and singled out any oxygen except from your booth.
Your smirk followed me to the flower markets,
into the night and my room,
waiting with the patient poisoned kiss in my
once-safe bed with a murderous gulp
of my minor heart.

The third bite

It finally sunk in,
as we commenced a musical war.
I battled over the track's latest analytics
and compared mine to yours.
I was holding on tightly
but I knew you'd speed-date managers soon.

You never liked competition
and I was a Belcher's Sea Snake.

The Final Bite

Why did you stay?

You released a sad song,
one of your hurt, pain and
the loss of the
"love of your life"

And it went viral.

I knew you'd find a manager soon
but I didn't expect an immediate effect.
I'm scared to lose this competition
especially since I knew your manager
hated me for representing you.

Now, it was different.

But the rivalry was still the same.

Why did you force yourself to stay
the whole time when your affair
had more memories of fun times
than those of ours?

Why didn't you leave?
I never stopped from choosing to go
but you didn't give me that choice
when you started smelling like her.

What was the point?
In pretending that you loved me
when you wanted to have her?

What was the point
in faking our dates as something more when your
musical lies didn't align with my musical truths?

What was the point if we weren't a team for life?

A heartache in disguise

Your innocent smile caught me off guard
the first night I saw you performing at the bar.
Your plain white tee and faded jeans,
hair slicked back with a small heart chain around your
neck.

You gave me that chain that night.

*"A family heirloom passed down generations to the next
love."*

It was love at first sight.
                              It was a heartache in disguise.
You were the performer,
                                      I was the director.
You were the player,
                                        I was the game.

Emotions manipulated

You put my heartbreak into a song,
garnering my album and singles
into a collective piece.

It became your "heartbreak".

You twisted my words,
changed the meanings,
rewrote the truths.

You told my story in another voice,
another perspective of falsity.
You disrespected my pain.

Your fans loved it.

I knew I couldn't compete with that
so I rested.
I ghosted my fans
to free myself
from the newfound creative block.

You manipulated emotions,
you manipulated hearts,
you manipulated words.

But security wasn't manipulated.

Haunted melodies

I played the key you despised.
I loved that key, but you refused to play any songs
in the key of F-sharp-minor.

Ironic? I thought not.

My newest single blew yours out of the water.
Haunted by my melodies, melodies you wasted.
The key of F-sharp-minor,
the key to our manipulated love.

Games with you

I played your musical game for too long.
My career wasn't in the music industry.
Never in the industry that ate me whole.

But my competition with you
was a game I never wanted to play.

Now my new album was about to release:

5...

4...

3...

2...

but it was still tainted by you.

You were the snake game

I hated snakes from a young age,
you only amplified that hatred by point-five
every
second.

My trembling hands

The thump-thump-thump on my apartment door woke
me.
Answering was the last thing on my mind,
eyelids heavy, half-drunk Cheval Blanc and scrunched
pages
scattered the floors.
You seldom had a messy workspace, but you were
persistent,
in more ways than one would've been resistant.
I hated the constant rhythmic percussion you created,
a song in my mind.

Midnight wasn't coming.
Let's try not to complicate it.
I didn't need a cricket at my
door.

Selfishly, the clicking of
your claws, probably too hard to admit
you couldn't let go of old ways to move
on.

My trembling hands opened the door,
your hair, wet from the rain,

and your white shirt stuck against your lean, muscular
frame.

I knew what you wanted
but your next words wrapped me like a constrictor.

Where was my happy ending?

"I want you back."

I, V, VI, IV.

You called me up and said you want me back.
You showed up drunk, undressed at my flat.
Her clothes scattered around my floor,
she called your name — I had my cricket bat.

Her sticky smell and your demon eyes
held my mind inside a light,
blinding me from everything
but the matte red — on your lips.

Another song composed,
another hit blasted through the charts.
I felt the constriction of you
running your fingers around my neck
and pressing tighter and tighter.

> *"You didn't want me back*
> *if you still sought her."*

I slammed the door

before I crashed into you.

Intoxicated

Alcohol began to impact my writing process.
Venom, reserved for composing songs —
never for fun, never to forget.

Intoxicated with words and drinks,
my hands played the chords.
This was a continuation of the story
far from a happy ending.

I consumed more wine than usual,
your presence repelled my concentration,
the key of G
trashed for D-minor.

I, VI, III, VII on repeat.

Sleep was a faraway ballad,
a lullaby sung to a stillborn.

A ballad of hearts.

Lost symphony

I noticed your single responding to my album
performed the worst of all your songs.
Social media has picked up on our past.
Scandals began to unfold
and your old fragrance was in the spotlight.

The world dimmed like those stage lights
when your world tour ceased.
The cheers of the crowd, unfading and powerful,
the shallow breaths,
        churning stomach,
            acid burning up my throat.
The release date was fast approaching,
my next album was still in shreds.
The symphony, intoxicated with memories of you.

Deceptive mastery

It was a smart move for your career,
but those fake lies poisoned my heart.

*"Aria,
relationships intrigued people.
That's why I wrote those love songs,
those breakup songs,
those emotional lyrics were everything to someone.
Everything they had to keep on living."*

It was the only way you kept living too.

Sweet venom

You weren't terrible at marketing yourself
once you incorporate your clever sorcery
of manipulation.
Your stage presence, beloved like snakes,
envisaged fear —
the fear of finding someone you couldn't lose.

Was she worth it?

"Lies of a Cheater"

The title of my album said it all.
These were the lies of a cheater,
the same man I let in twice,
who shed his skin but kept his core,
and realised who he was.

The man who created my music career.

"Lies of a Cheater" was out in the world
and the curtains were about to be undrawn.

One more single,
my goodbye to music forever.

True colours

Green hues revealed my album.
But I knew your attraction to the warm tones,
the red, orange and yellow album cover catching your
eye.

"You should've worn red lipstick.
It'd disguise your lack of beauty, aria."

"Blue made you look too pale,
wear the orange dress
so you don't embarrass me
in front of my fans."

"Pink roses?
You should've picked the yellow ones..."

I didn't do it out of petty feelings or revenge.
I wanted those songs to portray the truth
of my experience dating you.

"It was all someone had and needed to keep smiling."

I didn't release those songs to expose you.
I released them to let others know they weren't alone.
But you headlined in the final interview of the award
show
while I applauded with the acapella.

"Your Skin Didn't Shed"

Was my final single enough to silence you?
Was my final single enough to convince you?
Was my final single enough to help you?

Pages of a ballad

I kept those pages,
ballads you tried to write in F-sharp-minor.
You couldn't write them though I hoped one day you
would.
Your sad songs were my favourite pastime.
Then your love songs about us were a fleeting moment.

I haven't listened to your songs since.

I shredded those pages of a ballad
next to a shattered heart chain.

Suffocating memories

Tonight, I slept with dreams of everything we did.

The first dates, our first kiss,
my first red rose from you,
the first time you arrived home smelling like cheap
perfume,
the first red lipstick stain on your white tee,
the first love bite I never gave,
the first mention of another name in bed.

Those memories fogged my sleepy brain,
wiping away the fatigue that plagued me.
You were a flickering light during rehearsal,
one that stayed for a while and then blown.

The world sounded happier without you.

The final chord

I recalled playing the final chord of "Your Skin Didn't
Shed"
and feeling the whole song vibrate through my veins.
I remembered the enchanting lyrics,
the rush and the hubbub settled in my heart.

Songwriting was a friend and an enemy of mine,
but nothing faulted the perfection of this single.

And it was the final chord that brought it home.

My last breath

It was the last time I needed to fight for air.
The last time I would have seen you around.
I finally felt the closure I needed,
and chose to move and live in my favourite city.

I didn't have to fight for my last breath
like I fought for the last breath I took with you.

The final bite

You took the final bite of my heart when I departed.
Your fangs were still in my heart
but I pulled them out the second before my plane left.
I didn't need you around anymore
and I didn't need a happy ending with you.
I was over this musical game
and your game itself.
Your songs were figments of a past
that lit flames around my heart
to burn for new beginnings and not the end.

The past was the past for a reason.
Something that made me who I am today
but it wasn't the thing that defined me or my next move.

You taught me things I never knew I'd learn
and I thank you for those months because now,
I was moving into my future —

a future without you and lies.

A future where I didn't have to feel your final bite.

Thank you for reading *A Strangled Heart*! If you enjoyed the book, I would be beyond grateful if you left a review on any platform of your choice.

Reviews are so beneficial for authors and each one helps!

Love always,
Isabella

Instagram:
@isabellajuanitalyn

TikTok:
@isabellajuanitalyn

YouTube:
www.youtube.com/@isabellajuanitalyn

Acknowledgements

I never imagined that composing one song would lead to this poetry collection. Like a fresh of breath air, this poetry collection inspired, changed and altered my plans in more ways than I could count on both hands. And I am so happy that you were a part of this adventure.

This collection had a mind of its own and I am so grateful for every one of my readers, editors, illustrator and close ones for never once doubting this story.

Thank you so much to my lovely beta readers Talia, Olivia, Quindira, and Nancy for always being so supportive and excited to critique and help me make this book better than it was the first time I sent it to you. Your constructive criticism and attention to detail made this all possible. I am so thankful for such honest and compassionate friends who will go above and beyond to help me achieve my dreams!

To my proof editor Sopriya, thank you for catching those last-minute mistakes I never noticed! I am in awe with your attention to detail and the constant hype that you provided me with.

Thank you to Krystal for the wonderful illustrations that you conjured from my insane and messy drafts. I could never have brought this cover and design to life without your patience and amazing artistic talents.

As I mentioned, this book was never meant to become a book, but it did. And for that, I want to thank Mimi and her stuffed animal who I named Icy Pole for their continuous love, assistance and beautiful dedication as well as to staying up with me and hearing my little meltdowns every night.

I also want to thank James for always being there to help and for choosing the title from my crazy list. I am forever grateful to call you a friend and I am beyond thankful for your interest and creative assistance in finalising and bringing *A Strangled Heart* to life.

And finally, thank you to you, the reader, for showing this book so much love and adoration. I am continuously overjoyed by the constant happiness I receive. You deserve the world!

Love Always,
Isabella

Isabella Juanita Lyn is an author, poet, and digital creator. With a focus on love and heartbreak, her books contain heart-wrenching emotions to help others find themselves. She strives to aspire others to follow their dreams and most importantly, stand up for themselves and their beliefs. Besides writing, reading, and creating content, Isabella is obsessed with piglets and bunnies, learning random things in the world of Economics and Mathematics, and finding joy in life's little things.